T0381336

Collection of Expressions From The Heart

PAULA LYNN KUTCH

To order additional copies of this book, contact:
Xlibris
844-714-8691
www.Xlibris.com
Orders@Xlibris.com

ISBN: Softcover   978-1-4500-2434-1
          EBook   978-1-6641-4698-3

Print information available on the last page

Rev. date: 12/07/2020

I would like to dedicate this book to God, my Mother Esther and in loving memory of my father Paul Kutch. I would also like to thank George Brickhouse Jr. for helping me all of these years.

PAULA LYNN KUTCH